# CUSTARD AND PUPCAKE'S BOOK

## A Pet Pals Adventure

by Nicole Okaty

## Scholastic Inc.

New York  Toronto  London  Auckland  Sydney  Mexico City  New Delhi  Hong Kong  Buenos Aires

ISBN 0-439-70470-7

Designer: Emily Muschinske
Illustrations: Lisa and Terry Workman
Photographs: Nicole Okaty
Baylee Penny Hanright and Makenzie Nicole Allen
are pictured in the photos on pages 9 and 11.

12 11 10 9 8 7 6 5 4 3 2 1                                    5 6 7 8 9 10/0

Printed in the U.S.A.
First Scholastic printing, April 2005

# TABLE OF CONTENTS

# Get Ready for Strawberry Shortcake's Pet Pals Adventure!

Welcome back to Strawberryland, my berry sweet friend! You remember my two berry cute pets, Custard and Pupcake, don't you?

They are the most loving and lovable pets a girl could have! Together, we'll have a purr-fectly wond-**arf**-ul time—making yummy treats, playing pet games, and creating cat and dog projects! So grab your **Pet Craft Kit** and get ready for lots of coloring, cooking, painting, and pretend fun—with me and my two pet pals!

"Hi, there!"

"Woof!"

3

# Custard, Pupcake, and Strawberry Shortcake's Tips for Getting Started

1. Set up a space of your berry own where you can create your pet projects!

2. Whenever you see this picture throughout the book, it means that you can find what you need in your **Pet Craft Kit**.

3. Some of the materials you'll need can be found around your house. You can get other materials at your grocery or craft store.

4. Whenever you see this picture, you'll know to ask for help with some activities in the book.

## Origami, the Berry Basics

1. Origami is the Japanese art of paper folding.

2. To make the paper-folding projects in the book, use the square sheets of Custard-and-Pupcake-patterned paper found inside your **Pet Craft Kit**.

3. Take your time and follow each step closely.

4. To help make your folds crisp, you can use your fingernail.

## Getting Ready to Use the Kitchen

1. Inside your **Pet Craft Kit,** you'll find two berry cute cookie cutters. In the book, you'll get to bake yummy butter cookies with my two pets imprinted on them!

2. Before getting started, put on an apron and tie back your hair so that it doesn't get in your way—or in your food!

3. Wash your hands with soap and warm water.

4. Once you've chosen a recipe, get all of the ingredients and utensils together. Follow the step by steps.

5. Try to clean up as you cook, and put the ingredients away as you use them.

6. Always ask a grown-up for help when using utensils in the kitchen.

##  Getting Ready to Use Face Paints

1. Inside your **Pet Craft Kit,** you'll find 4 face paint crayons—pink, blue, white, and black—to paint your face (or a friend's face) to look like Custard and Pupcake.

2. The face paint crayons work best on a clean and dry face.

3. Berry important tip— keep the face paint away from your eyes!

4. Be berry careful to keep the face paint crayons away from your clothes because they may stain.

5. When you're finished with the paints, gently wipe your face clean with a tissue. Then wash your face with soap and warm water.

Turn the page for some cat and dog thumb-printing fun!

# Thumbprint Pets

*U*se your thumbprint to make one-of-a-kind cats and dogs!

## What You Need

- Pink and blue inkpad
- 1 sheet of white paper
- Black marker
- Small bowl of soapy water
- Paper towels

1. To begin, get the inkpad from your Pet Craft Kit. Use the pink side of your inkpad to make cats and the blue side of your inkpad to make dogs.

2. Which pet would you like to make first? Press your thumb on that color on your inkpad and then print it onto your paper. This will be your pet's body!

3. Using that same color, press just the tip of your thumb on the inkpad, and then print it toward the front of your first print. This will become your pet's head!

4. You can use the soapy water and paper towels, as needed, to clean your fingers after making prints with them.

5. To make cats, use your black marker to draw pointy ears on top of your pink print body. Add the cat's eyes, nose, mouth, and whiskers. Now add the cat's tail and legs. Use your imagination to make each cat a little different!

6. To make dogs, use your black marker to draw floppy ears on top of your smaller blue prints. Add the dog's eyes, nose, and mouth. Now add the dog's tail and legs. Use your imagination to make each dog one of a kind!

**Here's More:** You can draw cat and dog paw prints around your thumbprint pets. Use the inkpad in your Pet Craft Kit to print and draw paw prints of your favorite pets.

Turn the page to paint your face to look just like Pupcake or Custard!

7

# Fun Face Paints

Who do you want to look like first: Pupcake or Custard?

Please refer to Getting Ready to Use Face Paints on page 5.

1. **Which pet will you be? To color your face like Custard, take the pink, white, and black face paint crayons from your Pet Craft Kit.**

## What You Need

* Face paint crayons (pink, blue, black, white)
* Tissue
* Soap and warm water

2. **Using your white face paint crayon, make a circle around your mouth and nose. Color the circle in white—outline it in black, if you like.**

**3.** Make an upside-down triangle shape on the tip of your nose and color it in pink.

**6.** Make a blue circle around your left eye. Now draw a circle on the end of your nose and color it in blue. What other colors or details will you add—maybe a pink smile? You decide.

**4.** Add pink whiskers, if you like. What other details will you draw? It's up to you!

**Custard Face**

**Pupcake Face**

**5.** To paint your face like Pupcake, take the blue and pink face paints from your Pet Craft Kit.

*Here's More:* Will you bark and roll over like playful Pupcake or meow and groom your fur like princess Custard?

Turn the page to make perky animal ears that you can add to your face paint pets!

# Perky Pet Ears

You can dress up like my adorable pet pals in these perky pet ears!

1. **Ask a grown-up to help you cut out a 24-x-2¼-inch strip of white paper. The strip of paper needs to be long enough to wrap around your head, with a couple of extra inches for taping it.**

2. **Which pet ears would you like to make first? To make Custard's ears, cut out triangle shapes using pink paper. To make Pupcake's ears, cut out floppy shapes using blue paper— and fold down. Add pink to the inside of either pet's ears, if you like.**

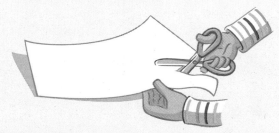

## What You Need

- 24-x-2 ¼-inch strip of white paper (poster board, medium-sized paper bag)
- Pink and blue construction or patterned paper
- Scissors
- Glue stick
- Tape

3. **Glue the ears evenly in the center of your strip of paper to make your pet headband.**

4. **Will you add some blue paper spots for Pupcake and pink triangles for Custard? It's up to you!**

5. **Hold the strip of paper on your forehead. Pull it back right above your ears. Ask a grown-up to measure and then tape the headband so that it fits securely on your head.**

*Here's More:* You can dress up like one of Strawberry Shortcake's berry cute pets! To dress up like Pupcake, wear a blue T-shirt or white T-shirt with blue paper spots taped on it. To dress up like Custard, wear a pink solid or pink patterned T-shirt.

Turn the page to see how you can make Custard out of folded paper!

# Clever Custard— Origami Cat

*You* can make my kitty cat, Custard, with just a few simple folds!

1. **To make Custard's head, fold a square of pink-striped paper on the diagonal. It will look like a triangle.**

2. **To make Custard's ears, fold down each of the top corners. There will be a point at the top.**

3. **Fold each ear up. Try to fold them evenly.**

## What You Need

- 2 sheets of pink-striped origami paper
- 2 extra sheets of paper— because it's fun to do the project with a friend
- Black marker
- Tape or glue stick

=

**4.** Fold down the point on the top of Custard's head. Fold up the tip on her chin.

 =

**5.** Turn the paper over. Using your black marker, draw Custard's eyes, nose, and mouth. Add some whiskers, if you like.

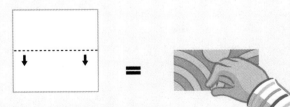

**6.** To make Custard's body, fold another sheet of pink-striped paper in half.

**7.** Stand the paper up—so that it looks like a tent. Use tape or a glue stick to attach Custard's head to her body.

Here's More: After you've made Playful Pupcake (see pages 14–15), your origami pets can have a berry fun time playing together!

# Playful Pupcake— Origami Dog

This perky puppy is always ready to play!
See if you can make Pupcake sit and stay.

1. **To make Pupcake's head, fold a square of blue-spotted paper on the diagonal. It will look like a triangle.**

2. **To make Pupcake's ears, fold down each of the top corners.**

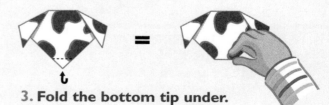

3. **Fold the bottom tip under.**

14

4. Using your black marker, draw Pupcake's eyes, strawberry-shaped eye patch, nose, and mouth. Add eyebrows, if you like.

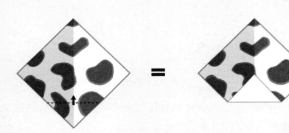

5. To make Pupcake's body, use another sheet of paper. Fold it on the diagonal like in step 1. Unfold the paper. Lay it flat so the fold goes from top to bottom. Fold the tip up about 1 1/2 inches, as shown in the picture.

6. Fold up both sides evenly, as shown.

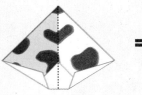

7. Fold the paper along the diagonal so you can see Pupcake's spots.

8. Use tape to attach Pupcake's head to his body. Tug out his tail a little.

9. Stand the paper up so you can make Pupcake sit and stay.

Turn a paper bag into Pupcake on the next page!

# Pupcake's Paper Bag Puppet

This adorable puppet is a bagful of fun!

1. Lay a small paper bag flat on your workspace with the bottom section facing up.

## What You Need

- Small paper bag or lunch bag
- Scraps of Pupcake-colored paper (blue, white, and pink)
- Scraps of Custard-colored paper (pink, white, and green)
- Scissors
- Glue stick or white craft glue

2. Cut out ears, eyes, spots, and a nose freehand from blue paper. Will you make Pupcake's ears teardrop shaped? Will his spots be different sizes? Will you add a white tummy? It's up to you!

3. You can make a light-colored patch around Pupcake's eye by cutting out a larger circle shape. Glue the smaller circle (eye) onto the larger circle (patch).

4. Glue Pupcake's ears, eyes, and nose onto the bottom section of the paper bag, as shown. Glue his spots on anywhere you like.

5. To use your Pupcake puppet, slip your hand inside the paper bag. Open and close the flap to make it look like Pupcake is barking.

Here's More: You can also make a Custard paper bag puppet. Once you do, you can put on a puppet show starring Pupcake and Custard. Will your pets bow wow and meow? Have fun making up voices for your pets and creating adventures for them.

Turn the page to make more cute pets.

# Custard and Pupcake's Pet Rocks

*You can make and take your pet rocks anywhere you go!*

## What You Need

- 2 well-shaped stones or rocks
- Small bowl of water
- Paper towel
- Paint (white & pink)
- Markers (pink, blue, green, black)
- Paintbrush
- Pencil
- Pink and blue construction or patterned paper
- Tape or white craft glue

1. Find two well-shaped smooth stones or rocks from outside. Wash the stones with water and dry them with a paper towel. Which pet would you like to make first—Custard or Pupcake?

2. Get the white and pink paint pots from your Pet Craft Kit. With a paintbrush, brush on the base color for your pet's face. Use white paint for Pupcake and pink paint for Custard. Let the paint dry. Use a pencil to sketch your pet's eyes, nose, and mouth.

3. Once you get your drawing the way you like, trace over the outlines with your black marker. You can use white paint for around Custard's nose and mouth, the green marker for her eyes, and the pink marker for her tongue.

5. Draw your ears with a pencil. Then cut the shapes out and tape or glue the ears to your pets.

4. To make ears for your pet, use blue paper for Pupcake and pink paper for Custard. You can make pointy ears for Custard and floppy ears for Pupcake.

Turn the page to have fun with your pet pals!

19

# Pet Pals Puzzle

This colorful puzzle is fun to put together. Berry best of all, you can play with the puzzle as many times as you like!

## What You Need

🍓 Strawberry Shortcake and Pet Pals puzzle

1. **Place the puzzle pieces from your Pet Craft Kit on a flat, hard surface—like a tabletop or the floor.**

2. **Begin by putting the outside pieces together, until you have formed the pink frame for your puzzle.**

3. **Continue to put together the puzzle—piece by piece—until all of the pieces are in place and the picture is complete!**

4. **Now you can take the puzzle apart and put it back together again—as many times as you like!**

Berry Funny

Q: What is more clever than a talking cat like Custard?

A: A spelling bee.

Here's More: You can cover your completed puzzle with a thin coat of puzzle glue or white craft glue. You can tape the back of the puzzle together with clear packaging or sturdy tape to keep the pieces in place permanently. Then you can display the puzzle in your room to remind you of your Pet Pals Adventure!

Turn the page to play a game where you search for Custard and Pupcake!

# Pet Pairs

Can you find all the Custard and Pupcake pairs? Look carefully—both pets must be doing exactly the same thing to make a match! Hint: There are 6 exact pairs.

Turn the page to see how good you are at knowing cats and dogs!

# Which Pet Am I?

Custard and Pupcake have come up with some berry fun facts about cats and dogs for this game. Can you figure out which pet is which—a cat or a dog—from the 10 clues given below?

1. I am called man's best friend.

2. I walk on my toes.

3. I like to have friends—both animal and human—to play with.

4. I spend almost half of my day grooming myself.

5. I get berry excited when I meet new people.

6. I usually prefer to be the only pet.

7. I am a famous _____ . My name is Snoopy.

8. I spend most of my day taking naps. I can sleep about 16 to 18 hours a day.

9. I like to play throw and fetch.

10. I squeeze my eyes closed when I am happy.

Turn the page to make some yummy
Custard and Pupcake cookies!

25

# Custard and Pupcake's Berry Best Butter Cookies

These berry yummy butter cookies are Custard and Pupcake's favorite. Can you guess why?

## What You Need

- Custard and Pupcake cookie cutters
- 1 cup (2 sticks) butter, softened
- 1 cup sugar
- 1 egg
- 1 ½ teaspoons of vanilla extract
- 2 ½ cups all-purpose flour (plus extra for rolling the dough)
- ¼ teaspoon salt
- Optional: Red and blue food coloring, parchment paper
- Utensils: Measuring cups and spoons, large bowl, electric mixer, rolling pin, cookie sheet, oven

Makes: 10 berry cute cookies (5 Custard and 5 Pupcake)

1. Ask a grown-up to preheat the oven to 350 degrees. You can line your cookie sheet with parchment paper so that your cookies don't stick. In a large mixing bowl, ask a grown-up to combine the sugar, butter, vanilla extract, and egg with an electric mixer. At medium speed, beat the ingredients until creamy.

2. At low speed, mix in the flour and salt.

26

3. Separate the dough in half. Place each half on parchment paper or a well-floured surface.

4. Add about 5 drops of red food coloring to color half the dough pink. Add about 5 drops of blue food coloring to color the other half blue. Knead both mixtures until each color is blended. Your dough may turn out a different shade of pink or blue rather than exactly matching the cookie cutter colors for Pupcake and Custard. Add more drops of food coloring to make your cookies deeper pink or blue.

5. Roll the dough out about ¼-inch thick on a well-floured smooth surface. Sprinkle flour onto the cookie cutters in your Pet Craft Kit so that the dough doesn't stick to them. Press firmly to cut the cookies out.

6. Place the cookie dough shapes on a cookie sheet about 1-inch apart and bake them at 350 degrees for about 10 minutes, or until the edges are golden brown. Let the cookies cool. Share them with your berry best friends!

Turn the page to see just how cute a Pupcake cupcake can be!

# Pupcake's Cupcakes

Pupcake loves cupcakes! That's how he got his name. You can decorate these no-bake cupcakes to look like my doggie.

## What You Need

- 3 vanilla cupcakes and 3 chocolate cupcakes (or 6 of one or the other)
- Buttercream frosting or your favorite light-colored frosting
- Fruit topping ideas: Blueberries, pineapple, mandarin oranges, strawberries, grapes
- Candy decorations: Round colorful candies, sprinkles, mini chocolate chips or chocolate bars, gumdrops, red hots, licorice
- Frosting or decorating pens

Makes: 6 cute cupcakes

1. **Pick your favorite kind of cupcake to decorate. Will you choose vanilla, chocolate, or both?**

2. **Buttercream frosting tastes berry yummy on both chocolate and vanilla cupcakes! Or you can use your favorite light-colored frosting on both the chocolate and vanilla cupcakes.**

**3.** Select fruit and candy toppings by their shape, color, and size to make Pupcake's face.

**5.** Use your imagination and have fun making your cupcakes look like Pupcake!

Chocolate Cupcake

Vanilla Cupcake

**4.** Will you make a strawberry licorice smile for your pup? Will you add round candy eyes and chocolate bar ears? You decide.

Strawberry Shortcake's Baking Tip:
I like fruit toppings best on vanilla cupcakes and candy toppings on chocolate cupcakes.

Turn the page for a berry creamy treat!

# Breakfast Berries 'n' Cream

Custard and I love to make this berries and cream recipe for breakfast! It's berry-licious!

1. **Put ½ cup of granola into a small bowl.**

## What You Need

- ½ cup granola or crunchy cereal
- ¼ cup light cream
- 5 raspberries
- 10 blueberries
- Optional: Strawberries
- Utensils: Measuring cups, small bowl, spoon

2. **Pour ¼ cup of light cream on top of the granola.**

3. **Add 5 raspberries and 10 blueberries, as shown. Will you add strawberries, too? It's up to you!**

4. **Eat your breakfast berries and cream with a spoon!**

**Here's More:** You can freeze some of your favorite berries in plastic baggies to make a berry creamy dessert!
When ready, place a mixture of your favorite frozen berries in a pretty dish, and then top with a spoonful of whipped cream. Berry-licious!

Turn the page to make "funny feline faces with food." See if you can say that 4 times berry fast!

## What You Need

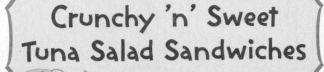

- Six-ounce can white tuna, drained
- 1 stalk of celery, finely chopped
- 2 tablespoons of mayonnaise
- 1 tablespoon of sweet relish
- Salt and pepper to taste
- 2 slices of bread
- Decoration ideas: Cheddar or other cheese, black olives, carrots, cucumbers, celery, sweet pickles
- Utensils: Can opener, measuring spoons, cutting knife, cutting board, fork, spoon, glass or cup, medium-sized bowl

Makes: 2 cat-faced sandwiches

# Crunchy 'n' Sweet Tuna Salad Sandwiches

Custard loves these tasty tuna treats, and so do I (and so will you)!

2. **In a medium-sized bowl, separate the tuna into smaller chunks using a fork.**

1. **With a grown-up's help, carefully open the can of tuna and drain the water.**

3. **Wash the stalk of celery in cold water. Ask a grown-up to chop the celery finely on the cutting board.**

**4.** Add the chopped celery, mayonnaise, sweet pickles, and salt and pepper to the tuna mixture. Mix well.

**5.** Using a glass or cup, stamp out a round circle in each slice of bread.

**6.** Spoon the tuna salad onto the circle-shaped slices.

**7.** Add decorations like sliced cheese, sweet pickles, olives, and veggies to make funny feline faces.

**Here's More:** You can use cookie cutters to cut out different-shaped sandwiches too! Custard likes to make fish-shaped sandwiches, for example!

Turn the page to sculpt my berry sweet doggie out of marshmallows!

# Marshmallow Pupcake

This delightful doggie can look like Pupcake and is made out of fluffy marshmallows.

## What You Need

- 2 big well-shaped marshmallows
- 9 mini marshmallows
- 6 round-tip toothpicks
- Blue and red icing writers or decorating gels
- Scissors (optional)

1. To make Pupcake's ears, ask a grown-up to cut or break a toothpick in half. Place one mini marshmallow on each rounded end of your toothpick.

2. Press the mini marshmallow stick ears into the top of a marshmallow head. Will you make one ear standing up and another to the side? You decide.

3. To make Pupcake's front legs, you'll need two toothpicks. Place two marshmallows on one end of each toothpick. Press Pupcake's front legs into the bottom of the marshmallow, as shown.

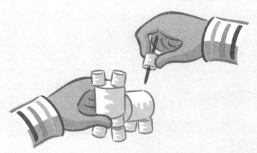

4. To make Pupcake's back legs, ask a grown-up to cut or break another toothpick in half. Place one mini marshmallow on each rounded end of your toothpick.

6. To make Pupcake's tail, place a mini marshmallow on the tip of a toothpick and press the mini marshmallow stick (marshmallow first) into the backside of the marshmallow.

7. Use blue icing writers or decorating gels to draw Pupcake's face and spots. You can also add his red tongue. It's up to you!

5. Attach the two marshmallows (the doggie's head and body) together using a toothpick, as shown.

Turn the page to make a house for Marshmallow Pupcake.

35

# Pupcake in His Doghouse

This delicious doghouse is made with peanut butter, graham crackers, and banana. You can play with your food and then eat it as a snack!

## What You Need

- Creamy peanut butter or other nut butter
- 10 graham cracker squares or sheets
- ½ banana, sliced in berry thin circles
- Utensils: Butter knife, plate

1. **Carefully break 5 graham cracker sheets in half to make 10 squares. (You'll only need 9 squares to build the doghouse, so go ahead and eat the extra cracker as a snack.) Spread creamy peanut butter onto 3 squares and make sandwiches by placing 3 more squares on top. You'll have 3 peanut butter sandwiches to use as walls for your doghouse.**

2. **To make the walls for your doghouse, stand the 3 sandwiches up, as shown. Use peanut butter to stick the sides together.**

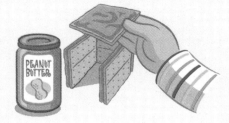

3. **Take another graham cracker square and spread peanut butter onto one side. Place the square on top of your doghouse walls, peanut butter side up.**

6. **Carefully break the last graham cracker square in half to make rectangle-shaped doors for your doghouse. Use peanut butter to stick the doors onto the front of your doghouse, as shown.**

4. **Spread peanut butter onto another graham cracker square. Carefully break it into two rectangles. Prop up the two crackers (peanut butter side up) to make a triangle-shaped roof.**

Here's More: You can place your marshmallow doggie inside Pupcake's Happy Home!

5. **Place banana slices on top of the roof for decoration.**

# Custard and Pupcake's Answer Page

## Pet Pairs (Pages 22-23)

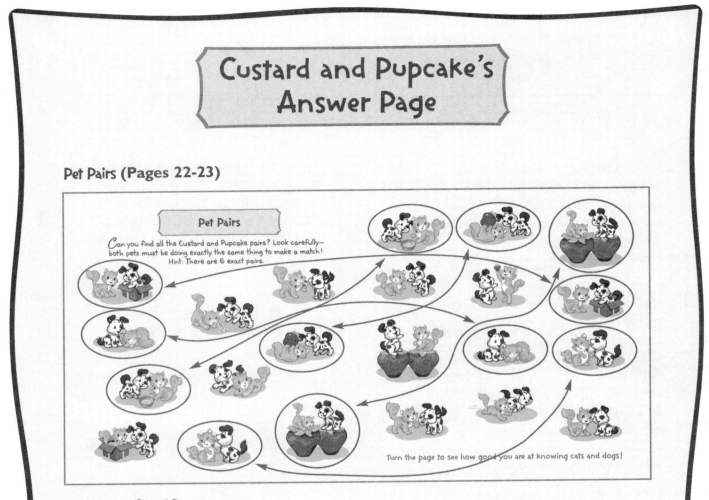

### Pet Pairs

Can you find all the Custard and Pupcake pairs? Look carefully—both pets must be doing exactly the same thing to make a match! Hint: There are 6 exact pairs.

Turn the page to see how good you are at knowing cats and dogs!

## Which Pet Am I?

### (Page 24)

1. Dog
2. Cat
3. Dog
4. Cat
5. Dog
6. Cat
7. Dog
8. Cat
9. Dog
10. Cat

# More Sweet
## Strawberryland Adventures
# COMING SOON!

To Our Berry Fun Friend,

Custard, Pupcake, and I hope you had fun on our Pet Pals Adventure. You can continue to create pet projects of your berry own using your imagination and your Pet Craft Kit. Remember, in Strawberryland it's a whole lot of fun to make crafts, share sweet treats, and play great games together. Until our next adventure!

Poodle-ooh,

Strawberry Shortcake

🐾 Custard, and Pupcake 🐾